The Beautiful Disruption

A Soul Story

GG Renee Hill

ISBN: 1492989851
ISBN 13: 9781492989851

Welcome: A Note from the Author.

Recently, I realized that I'm not crazy.

Creative, but not crazy.

An introvert with a demanding imagination, but still not crazy.

Being a highly sensitive and emotional person without a creative outlet is a scary way to live.

There's nowhere for the intensity to go.

I existed this way for years, constantly surrounded by people, trying to keep up, trying to seem normal, trying to align myself with their truths instead of discovering my own, while inside I was fading away.

My mind was filled with self-loathing, and I was always anxious and worried, certain that I was not emotionally strong enough to handle my life.

I got some professional help, I started writing, and I have not stopped since.

I changed the story I had been telling myself about "crazy in my blood" and "dysfunction in my mind."

Yes, my mother suffers from mental illness, but I don't.

Yes, for years I was depressed, anxious, paranoid, and self-destructive but now I'm not.

I'm truly thankful. But I still have my issues.

I wrote The Beautiful Disruption, a combination of reality and fiction, to put a creative frame around my inner conflicts, hoping that other women will find pieces of themselves in these pages.

It is a soul story, written in free verse, about a woman facing an interruption in her life.

You will explore her stream of consciousness and the landscape of her emotions thoroughly, as she seeks to find meaning in her struggles.

She has reached the point where her fear of self-discovery and change is eclipsed by her fear of stagnation.

From a whisper to a roar, her avoidance has caught up to her and she can no longer pretend she doesn't care.

She is ready to face herself and change her life.

As you read her story, I encourage you to ask yourself the tough questions and explore the parts of you that you have been afraid to explore.

The intensity—the contradictions and extremes that are hard to accept and harder to love.

When we don't understand this energy, we misdirect it into negative thinking, unhealthy relationships, bad spending habits, drugs, alcohol and other vices.

We find ourselves reflexively doing the same hurtful things, thinking the same painful thoughts—"I'm crazy! I'm not good enough! I have bad luck!"—over and over and over again, unconsciously making our nightmares come true.

But when we learn to embrace the beauty of who we are and what we have been through—pain and pleasure, enlightenment and foolishness—that is when we truly begin to thrive.

Prologue: She Contradicts Herself.

She is an idealist.

She believes in the dream, the helpers, the comfort of love speak and the power of feelings exchanged in silence and rhythm.

She also has a dark side, a critic, determined to hold her hostage.

Questioning her at every turn, she tries to stay one step ahead, but still she wanders, intrigued by shadows.

She doesn't deny the dark side its benevolence.

It informs her by contrasting and shaping things, revealing her whole soul.

She doesn't believe in enemies, within or without.

Everything is for her deeper perspective.

Intense cravings and instincts challenge what she's been taught.

Everything she thinks she knows is stored in the recesses of her mind, pending exploration, waiting to be judged.

She is an accidental artist, aroused by the complex and uncertain, determined by intention.

Peace, her quiet muse, hides in her labyrinth just waiting to be discovered.

She stands by her convictions, for better or worse and she makes willful sacrifices to test them.

Her biggest fear is living a default life, never breaking through.

An innate curiosity to dig up, explore and find out feeds her relentless cravings.

She is full of joy and fear, a potent cocktail of emotions.

She was raised to care about right and wrong, good and bad, heaven and hell.

But her heart has always drawn her toward a broader reverence, forcing her to find out for herself.

If she had been Eve, she would have tasted the forbidden fruit and relished it, preoccupied with sensation as the sky fell down around her.

She thrives in her sensitivities, indulging in the wealth of energies that life has to offer.

Employing every aspect, every peculiarity, every heartbeat toward being who she is here to be.

She's one step ahead; then she's stumbling, falling behind.

Expecting the worst, claiming it before it can claim her.

Both strange and familiar, her habits disrupt, evolve, and repeat, disrupt, evolve, and repeat, until she finally dares to confront them.

She is a woman in transition.

Her story is both anecdotal and deliberate, designed to spark your imagination and turn on your resonance so you can see parts of yourself that have been suppressed.

Her circumstances, alive with individual and collective truth, remind us that everyone's path is unique and significant.

She is young enough to wonder and dream, old enough to plan and protect.

She is gracious, self-conscious and watchful.

She stands with outward composure and inner doubt.

Magnetic, surrounded by love that she can't help but attract.

She prefers to go unnoticed but she craves attention and indulgence.

A curious, vibrating soul, she is at odds, but never against herself, for she is always better for the tangled journey.

This is the story of her disruption.

The Beautiful Disruption

She Wakes Up Abruptly.

There is a tightness in her chest and a cramp in her gut.

After staring at the alarm clock for seconds that feel like hours, trying to comprehend the red numbers on the screen, she jumps up realizing she is late for work.

Reality is like a fog, just on the edge of her consciousness, blurring her reflection in the mirror, giving her a distorted look.

She has to keep moving.

No time to fall apart now.

She resists the fog until she gets in the car.

The cramp in her gut has dissolved into butterflies and she feels lightheaded.

She tries to gather herself into one feeling that will simplify everything.

Slowly she allows the events of the last week to replay in her mind.

The truth almost comforts her with its creeping return, but in a sick way, like a fix to an addict.

It hurts so good.

Because she knew.

She knew all along, and finally she has proof.

He cheated.

Everything she knows about herself is swallowed up by his betrayal.

Her feelings are a virtual mind map in her head, triggering thoughts and assumptions that she can't control.

His sin is her scarlet letter.

Her humiliation on display.

She'd believed in him when her instincts told her to question.

Her embarrassment leads her to anger.

He endangered her with his greediness.

He lied.

He laughed recklessly when she confronted him.

Accused her of bringing this on herself.

His dark heart revealed.

Her anger leads to fear.

No protection.

Her body and spirit exposed to deception.

Intimacy contaminated.

His indifference terrifies her, but worse, her failure to protect herself.

She feels like her own starry-eyed enemy.

Her fear leads to suffering.

He called the other woman his love.

He came to her for his good mornings and good nights.

He held her, wanted her, and moaned when he entered her.

Images float, and agony squeezes and won't let go.

Her suffering leads to sadness.

Finally, the tears come.

She can't get the words and pictures out of her mind.

She realizes that she has arrived at work, in the parking garage, in the parking space, in the car, where they'd laughed, kissed, loved and fought.

He is in all her places, inside and out and she cannot escape him.

She looks in the mirror at her reflection, blurry from tears, blurry from the fog of her reality and she takes a deep breath and releases it.

Slowly coming into focus, she sees that she is still there.

Altered, but still there.

Tissue, powder, eyeliner, lip gloss.

Breath, prayer, courage, faith.

She gets out of the car and walks into the building, bruised and beaten but not broken.

> *I can't fall apart*, she says to herself. *I have to keep going*.

She Had A Premature Knowledge of Crisis.

Her childhood was shaped by chaos and love.

Adored and overprotected, she was taught to study, fear God and be quiet.

Her mother heard voices that no one else could hear and saw things that no one else could see.

After a while, her mother's instability accumulated and over-lapped until there was no way to see past it.

No one addressed it.

Self-appointed, she was the one who minded the gaps.

Cleaned up the messes.

Apologized.

Got lost in managing her mother's extremes.

She felt responsible for her mother's behavior and handily designed her existence to compensate for it.

She wanted people to feel comfortable all the time, even at her own expense.

Being a pleaser gave her a purpose, a reason to take up space and be less of a burden.

Something is wrong with me, she decided early on.

She created a story about a broken girl with a broken mother who would grow up to live a broken life. She chose that fate and lived according to it.

Resentful, but kind.

Polished, but cracked.

Full of secrets, she became a representative character, busy with lies to remember and images to keep up.

An artificial escape, based on what she thought people wanted her to be.

Everything was fragile, hanging on a thread, unhealthy.

This viral depression diminished her.

Dread was always with her, an alarm system in her head, alert to her next disaster.

Despite being resigned to a life of misfortune, she became resourceful.

She grudgingly noticed that things always worked out, even when she claimed defeat.

An inconvenient truth, yet it was right there, in her face, betraying her self-punishments and assumptions.

She kept overcoming things, dammit, aggravating herself.

She still felt so much joy, despite her efforts to be miserable.

Her life was full of miracles and spectacles that she was afraid to rely on so she didn't know how to enjoy, how to be thankful, without guilt.

She didn't want to win and she didn't want to lose.

Ambiguity intrigued her and she found passion in the gaps between hope and despair.

She is Part of A Cycle.

Mothers. Grandmothers. Sisters. Friends.

Living in a compromised state, repressing painful thoughts, and wearing an impenetrable mask every day, just to get by.

Her denial started when she found herself making up lies to hide her mother's erratic behavior.

As she got older, she continued to lie, pretend, conceal, about everything, at all costs, to avoid being seen and judged.

Her mother and her mother's mother taught her what they knew, to enable her survival.

But the tools for self-worth got lost along the way as they sacrificed their own sensibility to get by, to feel love.

Her budding notions of self-image were soiled, as shame began to exceed joy.

Commonly labeled as too light, too dark, too nappy, too curvy, too mouthy, too nice, too curious, too peculiar, too artsy, too nerdy, too broke, too prissy, too ghetto, too much, too little; soon she began to value herself and her world based on this critical posture.

Now, instead of looking in the mirror and celebrating her unique beauty, instead of looking inside and appreciating her intensities, she sees all of the labels and criticism that she has absorbed over the years.

She overcompensates and hides her perceived flaws until the day comes that she doesn't recognize the woman in the mirror.

Identity crisis.

Seeking solace in everything from drugs to alcohol to sex.

Nothing gets her high enough or satisfied enough to ignore her pain and confusion.

A highly sensitive person, without a creative outlet—a dangerous way to live.

She has this yearning, this craving for freedom, a perspective that gives her a voice; but she has insecurities and doubts that hide that voice away.

She wants to break this cycle but she doesn't think she is strong enough.

Only now that her world seems to be falling apart does she realize that she is not the same as her mother.

She hears voices too, but they tell her that she is whole, that she is strong and that she can trust herself.

Despite this empowering guidance, she fears that she will choose badly, a victim of destiny and composition.

She doesn't believe in herself.

Burned bridges and bad decisions.

Might as well dance on the edge, tempt the fall.

She Wonders if Her Eyes Betray Her Smile.

She greets the security guard, takes the back staircase up to her floor, to her office, and closes the door.

Routine takes the wheel as she starts up her computer and stares at the screen.

So tired.

Tired of covering up and pretending to be happy.

Tired of giving too much and not requiring enough.

Tired of knowing better and not doing better.

> *Is life supposed to be this hard or do I just make everything more difficult because I am me?*

He cheated, yes.

But she cheated herself.

It's not just about his unfaithfulness or his indifference.

The deepest pain comes from her own betrayal.

She's been unfaithful to herself so many times, allowing herself to be mistreated.

And when given the chance to escape, she would always go back for more.

Chasing chaos.

She's been dismissed.

Lied to.

Unappreciated.

Betrayed.

Disrespected.

Devalued.

And here, sitting at this desk, staring at this screen, eyes hot with tears, she is still not certain that she didn't deserve all of it.

When she is not sure of herself, and she never has been, she just lets whatever is happening—happen.

She allows herself to be influenced by what seems easiest in the moment.

She bends easily and lets the limitations and whims of others become her own.

She's cheated herself religiously, creating a clear path for others to take advantage.

She doesn't know why she keeps doing the same things.

Her unawareness does her choosing for her, almost as if she's on autopilot, watching herself with no control.

But wait. This is no surprise.

This self-denial is what she's always predicted for herself.

The beautiful sufferer.

Lost in extremes.

The broken girl with the broken mother who would grow up to live a broken life.

Her self-fulfilling prophecy of defeat.

A conscious decision that deep down she is no good and good things were not meant to happen to her.

Naturally, she attracts what she expects.

Yet, she's relieved that he's gone, even as she owns the defeat.

His dark heart.

Her resilient joy.

Somehow, she feels something more than just failure.

Something like hope is beckoning her, just as it always has.

Hope taps on her shoulder playfully, but when she turns, looking for evidence, no one is there.

Hope tickles her feet, making her dance when there's no music.

She can't yet define it or explain it and still, she believes in it.

When We Believe That We Are Meant to Suffer.

We attract situations that feed this belief.

Our relationships mirror our most intimate personal reflections of ourselves.

If we are empty, we can't fill ourselves up with someone and become full.

Or solve problems with the same logic we used to create them.

Or deny the parts of ourselves we don't like.

Or pretend we don't care when we do.

Or seek perfection over sincerity.

We can't make ourselves too responsible, trying to be everything to everyone.

We can't change the stories of defeat we tell ourselves without first embracing our underground, our secrets, the very source of these stories.

The underground is not a hopeless place.

It's the denial of it that weakens us, makes us feel incomplete and compromises our sense of self.

She has been looking everywhere but inside.

Inside—where original sin and worldly thoughts run rampant.

She was taught.

Deny.

Repress.

Deny.

Don't look into their eyes.

Don't look into your own soul.

Take what I feed you.

So she did.

She took what everyone fed her, eating to the point of excess.

And still, she is starving.

Like A Pouting Child.

She doesn't want to be seen but she craves attention.

She doesn't say much, but she envisions words seeping out of her and floating over her head, telling all her stories.

Her imagination is her buffer.

She moves through the day avoiding eye contact.

God forbid someone look her in the eye and ask if she is okay.

Floodgates compromised.

She doesn't want anyone to know but she's dying to tell.

Her suffering, her intentions, her dreams, her unconditional tolerance.

When she does talk, she rambles, struggling to stay detached.

Afraid of being discovered, trying to ignore all of the unstated feelings floating around her.

She feels peculiar and vulnerable, and she wonders what everyone else is going through.

On the way to grab lunch, she locks eyes with a passing stranger and she smiles at him in spite of herself.

He mirrors her smile.

For that brief moment, they understand and comfort each other.

How hard she falls for a beautiful moment.

A tender distraction.

She finds escape in watching people.

Her problems shrink when she considers the universe around her.

People are walking, talking, working, eating, crying, laughing, believing, loving, hating, suffering.

Living their own realities, reflections of their own minds.

She's just one in seven billion.

Seven billion people, seven billion stories.

She pictures the number fluctuating with birth and death, as her thoughts carry on.

She's engrossed with love and what it all means and how to pour it out.

How to be different and still be herself.

Why does she have to love so hard?

Think so hard?

Exist so extremely?

She aches, never wanting this kind of exposure again, fearing that her heart will break over and over and over, a slow leak with no chance to heal.

He cheated.

She is not surprised.

Life disappoints.

The sky falls.

Every day something new hurts and she can't ignore the foreboding.

No protection.

She feels like her own starry-eyed enemy.

She wants to be sharper, more focused, more practical.

Kill the dreamer.

Awaken the warrior.

As she sits on a bench, eating lunch, watching people come and go, she decides that this is happening so she can learn something about herself.

She knew this would come.

A turning point.

She wonders why she falls the hardest for men who mistreat her, situations that rip her.

Why the need for pain and uncertainty?

Is it a deeper instinct or a dysfunction? she wonders.

The beautiful sufferer.

She's mad that she sees herself this way and mad that she likes it.

She never chooses the easy, predictable route over a provocation.

She's wired for conflict.

Everything feels better when it is earned.

Her phone buzzes incessantly with texts and voicemails that she absentmindedly ignores.

Heavy with requirements, she shuts it all out to hold herself together.

Quiet makes more sense than noise as she is positioning things, making room for her new reality.

She has to make this count.

This disruption must have meaning.

The second half of the day won't wait for her, so she heads back to the office, proud of herself for making this bigger than him, more than just a breakup.

But now, even the briefest breeze of thought brings him back to mind and she misses him, longing once again for passion and escape.

She Loved Him.

But he didn't know how to love.

He could talk about love.

He could see love and feel love.

But he couldn't give love.

He could make love.

But he couldn't make promises.

She had desperately wanted his promises.

She wanted his heart, knew she couldn't have it so she took what she could get.

Temporary bliss.

Passionate highs and lows.

Withdrawal and manipulation.

He only stayed long enough to take what he needed and keep moving.

If he stopped moving, he would self-destruct.

If he stopped wandering, he would have to face himself.

He chose to stay in the dark where he couldn't see.

If he exposed himself and the sun came out, he'd see his shadow.

He was deathly afraid of his shadow.

She saw his shadow, loved it, understood it.

Saw potential in it.

She thought her love would change him.

He pushed and he pulled, tested boundaries, thinking she would never leave.

He knew he was hurting her, but he didn't know how to share anything but pain.

He was only comfortable in chaos.

Claiming souls before they could claim him.

Her love, her body, she had given to him and he'd taken with such feigned sincerity, absorbing every drop of her.

His dark heart concealed.

She'd let him enter her spirit and stroke her soul where everything is love and sensation and surrender.

Wide open, exposed to deception.

It had never occurred to her that this desire was not love.

It was blinding the way she wanted him.

She couldn't see what was really happening, only what she wanted to happen.

When she discovered his indiscretions, she threw love in his face and beat him with it.

Somewhere deep down, in her labyrinth, her intricacy, the darkest part of her soul, she relished the mayhem.

She felt a sense of privilege for having such passion in her life.

He stirred her core.

The place she dared not enter.

The place she could not stir for herself.

But something wasn't right.

His eyes were cold and dark.

His energy—unaffected.

He laughed at her and her antics, told her she was a mess.

Frantic, she looked for love hiding in his eyes, in his face, in his stance, and she found nothing but disdain.

And her heart stopped.

We Experience What We Create and We Attract What We Are.

An intuitive feeler, engaged with her world.

Self-conscious.

She's attracted to people who hurt like she hurts.

She's afraid of her own underground but she embraces the dark side in others.

She wants to fix, to make others comfortable in order to decrease her own burden.

She is waiting to be put together.

Waiting for instructions and permissions.

She can't tolerate discomfort so she enables bad habits— hers, his, everyone's.

Cooperation is love, after all.

Isn't it?

Won't it make people change?

Won't accepting and partaking in madness create a healing bond of love and devotion?

Something isn't right.

She's got it wrong.

Conflict and frustration abound.

She must not understand what love is really about.

She's attracted to his beautiful suffering because it is familiar.

She wants what he can teach her, by getting close to his fire and allowing herself to be burned.

She has to see, she has to know.

In seeking to heal him, in exploring his underground, she is really seeking to heal and explore herself.

Her Mother was Her First Love.

Her smell, her voice, her softness.

Her arms, the safest place on earth.

Their rituals molded her and made her tender.

She watched closely and loved her details, emulated her femininity.

Her sways, her grace, her secrets.

She hears her mother's voice reverberating in her own throat.

Her mother was the stimulant for a lifelong love of women, beauty and complexity.

Because of her, she is drawn to the wounded exquisite: love, pain, signs of contradiction and twists of mania.

She craves men but women are her most abiding lovers.

Her friends are her soul mates, all the love without the consumption of sex and romance, a different kind of intimacy.

Women make love by admiring each other, studying and envying each other and mixing it all up in a pot of devotion.

Their love is in the details.

When she's feeling her most stunning, they are the ones who truly see her, more than any man ever has.

They assemble each other based on the unspoken things.

The knowing acceptance.

The feeling of being witnessed and reflected effortlessly.

Easy to see and feel, hard to explain.

Women form a wall of solidarity—a force field of love and pain and protection.

It's a sparkle in the eye, a smile that knows tears, a hug that heals and warms.

She is Overstimulated
and Wants to Hide.

She stands back to observe her environment before she explores it.

The lobby is full of people walking in and out.

Lunchtime.

The stimulus of sound and movement and energy coming from every which way wears her down.

Everything seems hypermagnified and overlapping, and she wants to get back to her thoughts.

Work seems absurd when life is interrupted.

She sees the path of least resistance and makes her way through the crowd, looking intently at her feet to avoid eye contact.

But her friend has spotted her and stepped into her path.

Looking into her eyes, a concerned, *What's wrong?*

Oh no, the floodgates.

Seeing her tear up, her friend goes into protective mode and acts quickly, grabbing her hand and leading her to the back staircase.

By the time they reach her office, she has her tears under control, but her eyes still burn with shame.

His sin is her scarlet letter.

Her humiliation on display.

They sit down.

Her friend watches, waits, gives her space.

>   *It's done.*

Done? What happened?

>   *It doesn't matter, it's done.*

Okay. Are you sure you don't want to talk about it?

>   *He cheated. He's been cheating. Probably the whole time.*

Her friend nods. She knew this was coming. She watches, waits, gives her space.

I knew. I told myself that I was happy, but I wasn't. I knew all along that something wasn't right, but I wanted to fix him. I thought we could save each other. He told me that no one understood him and I knew that I could give him that acceptance. I just wanted him to believe in me, that I was good enough. I never felt like I was enough—for anyone. But if I could fix him, then that would prove to me that I was enough.

I brought out the best in him—he told me so. He told me that I have this light and that I had taken that light and lit up places inside of him that he'd forgotten about. That made me feel special and I believed him.

Long pauses in awkward places as she struggles to hold the floodgates.

Her words are half-decided, uncertain, searching.

I guess I just saw what I wanted to see. I could accept that he wasn't perfect, that we weren't perfect. But I just wanted him, like I was under a spell. He knew how to stroke me in every way, how to make me need him.

I thought it would pay off—my loyalty, you know? I would be the one who stuck by him no matter what he did. But the more I gave, the less he cared. I got clingy and needy, and he started calling less, making excuses all the time. I felt him slipping away and that just made me even more desperate. It was getting to the point where I could not stand to look at myself. I let him do whatever he wanted and I just waited and waited and waited. We didn't do my way, we did his way—always.

And then I caught him with her and I confronted him and his eyes were so empty. His laugh was so mean, like he never cared at all.

She shudders to release the toxic energy of her memory.

He's nonchalant about all of it. He doesn't care and I was stupid and now it's done. But thank God, because if he had shown any sign of caring, I think I would have forgiven him.

She chokes on her words, on her allowances and his lies, looking into her friend's eyes with desperation.

Silently, her friend opens herself up, letting the pain become a shared thing.

One witness, one testimony, one bond deepened.

She lays her head on her shoulder, and her friend holds her, forming a force field of love and pain and protection.

Attracted to Complexity and Contradiction.

She has lived most of her life feeling like a self-conscious paradox.

A little self-righteous and sheltered.

A little rebellious and damaged.

Only ever wanting to make peace with herself and be everything that she is without remorse.

An inner conflict, thinking that to accept one aspect is to deny another.

Instinctively, she yearns to connect and grow with people who embody her contradictions.

She knows that denying her underground hurts her, but she doesn't know how to indulge her dark side without losing herself to it.

She was taught.

Deny.

Repress.

Deny.

This delicious tension pulls her toward her journey.

She wants to understand what plagues her and what brings her peace, and she craves other souls who understand.

Clumsily, she stumbles along, feeling the push and pull of her contradictions.

Until there is a disruption.

A situation, a harsh indifference, that makes her realize that she can love and hate.

Rejoice and grieve.

Thrive and suffer.

Lie and tell the truth.

And still be whole.

Love Makes Pain Beautiful.

This is what her friend told her.

Her witness, who listened and shared her pain.

She's comforted by her words.

The look in her friend's eyes, the intensity of her presence, the quiet acknowledgment, the lack of judgment, the sounds of affirmation, the pot of devotion.

All this assures her that she will not float away or be swallowed up by confusion.

As she walks to her car, she is a child with a freshly cleaned, kissed, bandaged wound.

It still throbs, but feels better.

She won't bleed out, she won't die.

Love makes pain beautiful.

So suffering will be her teacher.

> *There is something on the other side of all this,* she said.

Soul deep, she feels movement.

Driving home, in her car, in her mind, she wanders and searches.

She recalls the story.

The one about the broken girl with the broken mother who would grow up to live a broken life.

It had never occurred to her to see things differently.

But here, in this moment, she knows that she is creating a new story.

Her sorrow feels slippery and dangerous and unsustainable.

Yet she still feels this pull, this hope.

And she believes in it.

She just doesn't know how to engage it.

This yearning, this craving for freedom, has a strong voice; but her insecurities and doubts have silenced it.

When she is not sure of herself, and she never has been, she just lets whatever is happening—happen.

Now, she wants to decide.

She wants to be deliberate, done battling with circumstance.

Backed into this strange, inevitable corner, she starts looking around.

Timidly, at first.

One step ahead, then stumbling, falling behind, anticipating her fear.

Deep in her shadows, she locates the false affirmations tattooed on her insides, spelling out her fate.

> *You aren't good enough. You don't deserve to be happy. You aren't special. You have crazy in your blood. You don't have what it takes. You mess everything up. You are destined to fail. You are not creative, insightful, or distinctive. You're a quitter. You are selfish. You are lazy. You have no backbone. You shatter easily. You don't deserve to win.*

Her insides are covered with hate and judgment.

She is frightened and intrigued.

She sees scary memories and sequences that illustrate her ugly thoughts.

Questions of morality and intention.

Layers and layers of self-denial, jealousy and resentment.

So harsh when isolated and stared at.

This is her labyrinth, her intricacy, the darkest part of her soul.

She looks around horrified, disgusted with herself.

But the more she drives, in her car, in her mind, in her underground, she wanders through her murkiness, through her discomfort and she starts to breathe a little easier.

She confronts herself without flinching or hiding or covering up and she sets her judgments aside.

Evoking unconditional, all-encompassing love, unleashed and spilling over, she decides that no matter what she finds within herself, she will love it and be gentle with it.

> *There's room for peace here. Dark and light can't exist without the other.*

She has always lived to let live.

She seeks to please, even at her own expense.

Her expense has been her freedom, her peace of mind, her value.

Now here is a new story, one that activates hope, despite all her previous efforts to be miserable.

She considers her life, full of miracles and spectacles that she's been afraid to rely on.

She feels foolish for not being more thankful.

She pulls into the driveway.

She can't remember the drive home.

She Saw the Slap Coming in Fast Slow Motion.

Her mother's face was contorted, eyebrows furrowed in anger and concentration, lips tucked in and braced for impact, her body jerking awkwardly with the effort.

This was a defense, not an attack.

Her mother felt threatened and she lashed out at her daughter the same way she did in her sleep when she was being assaulted by invisible forces.

She couldn't experience the whole thing in that moment; it felt more real in hindsight, once she'd had a chance to sit back and replay it.

It was the first and last time that she tried to convince her mother to see a doctor.

She was fifteen; her mother was sick, the kind of sick that no one talks about, and her father was at work.

Her mother had a persecution complex.

There was a widespread conspiracy to torment her, no one could tell her different, and she and her father were conspirators.

Every cupboard door that was left open, every placemat that was left crooked, every chair not pushed completely under the table was a thorn intended to puncture her.

She would try to explain.

This was her script: explaining, justifying, pacifying.

Her mother's gaze always condemned and eventually she began to question herself.

Maybe I am the crazy one?

Maybe she really *was* doing these things on purpose, under some sinister control that she was too brainwashed to recognize.

She wanted to be a good girl—in that childlike, definable way—but she was getting older and good was getting more complicated.

Her mother self-medicated with religion.

To be a teenager, with her instincts and urges, was a sin.

Deny.

Repress.

Deny.

She was taught that good people didn't sin and that bad people knew better but sinned anyway.

According to that, she was bad.

She *wanted* to be bad.

Her mother was right about her, it seemed.

Fifteen. Sixteen. Seventeen. Boys. Flirting. Kissing. Touching. Cursing. Sneaking.

She smoldered with emotion and rebellion, tucked away.

Hidden from her mother's reproach.

Dirty.

Raw guilt mixed with righteousness mixed with angst and paranoia created a dangerous cocktail in her mind.

She tried to gather herself into one feeling that would simplify everything.

All she could come up with was anger.

Someone had left the oven on.

She hadn't used the oven in days, so she knew it wasn't her.

It was three in the morning, and her mother had come into her bedroom, turning all the lights on, demanding answers.

Squinting. *I don't know, Mom. I didn't use the oven today.*

> *So are you saying that I left it on? I didn't use the oven today either; I used the stovetop. Who put you up to this?*

Feeling the anger bubble up in her stomach and work its way up to her chest and throat, she tried to stay calm. *Mom, no one! Can I go back to sleep?*

> *Not until you tell me what this is about! What do they want? Did they promise you something? Have they hurt you? What else did they tell you to do to me?*

Her mother rambled on about how they're all cowards, cowards and devils, and she'll be protected because she's on the side of God, and she won't let them take her family, and the book of Genesis says—

She interrupts.

> *Mom, this has to stop! Why do you do this? I'm your daughter. I'm not out to get you. I would never hurt you. No one is trying to hurt you or me or anybody! This is crazy! I don't understand what makes you think this way. You need to see a doctor! Something is wrong with you!*

Sobby, messy, spitty words.

Fight-or-flight adrenaline running through her made her want to punch something. And then, the slap.

Had she raised her hand to her mother? No.

Did her mother say she did? Yes.

The story would always be twisted.

Did she leave the oven on?

Did she take orders from someone to torment her mother?

Whose world was the real one?

So many wrinkles in her memory.

Ever Since Her Mother was Diagnosed with Schizophrenia.

She has been worried that she would face the same fate.

Caught up in a cycle.

Making up lies to hide her mother's erratic behavior.

Pretending and concealing, believing her own stories.

Everyone lies, everyone pretends not to see, so why shouldn't she?

Even before the diagnosis, there were obvious peculiarities common to her mother and maternal grandmother.

She didn't need a diagnosis to know that there was some kind of disjointed nuance passed down from mother to daughter.

With this awareness, she would look at herself in the mirror and feel hopeless.

Her lies delayed the inevitable.

She remembers her mother's episodes and how they consumed everything with their imminence.

There was never a certain moment, never a clean, clear day, never a chance to let her guard down.

She could not be herself in her own home, with her own mother, because she was always a suspect.

Still, she minded the gaps.

Cleaned up the messes.

Apologized for breathing and existing.

Escaped into her mind when her mother lashed out.

Got lost in managing her extremes.

She didn't think she had a chance.

By expecting the worst, she felt a warped satisfaction when things went wrong.

She chose to condemn happiness, rather than welcome the vulnerability it required.

She expected that if life ever found her too content, something terrible would happen to bring her back down.

She survived by hurting herself before she could be hurt.

To love life is to love freedom and be brave.

That persistent knowing.

Imperishable, despite her efforts to ignore it.

Life feels like a tightrope, and then it feels like a trampoline.

Steady. Bounce.

Steady. Bounce.

Look down. Don't look down.

Fly. Twist and turn. Be still.

She wants to hold on, and she wants to let go.

Remember and forget.

Every day, there is something to release.

Old ideas and limitations.

Sickness and loyalty.

Harsh words from people who don't know what else to say or any other way to be.

The mania of her mother.

Her smell, her voice, her softness.

The disruption of the man she loved—intimacy contaminated.

Guilt, beauty, laughter, irritation—they come and go; she feels, she clings, she suffers.

But the letting go consumes her with its necessity.

How is she to function when every moment, every happening, has the potential for another disconnection, another good-bye?

She believes in grieving in advance.

Misfortune comes suddenly, without pretense, so she never dares to be *too* happy.

Happiness feels like disrespect when there is so much to be sad about.

And yet, she feels this hope, this pull, and she believes in it, dammit; she always has.

She feels hope, even when the earth is swallowing her up.

That must mean something.

She trusts it.

He told her once that she had this light and that she had taken that light and lit up places inside of him that he'd forgotten about.

Now she must do that for herself.

Days Without Pain.

Laughter without sorrow.

Sun without rain.

None are promised.

Every extreme has the potential to expand us and make us more aware of what *is*.

Even our most intense challenges, the monsters that linger with us, our painful memories.

They are necessary for us to be the whole entity that we are supposed to be.

She doesn't believe in enemies, within or without.

Everything is for her deeper perspective.

Highs come with lows, mistakes come with success and pleasure comes with pain.

She is finding the connections.

Her childhood. Her mother. Her now.

She sees herself trying to prove something about her intentions, her fundamentals and she sees her efforts in vain.

See me! See me!

Her voice is tired after screaming for years with no sound.

She wanted her mother to love her enough to stop being schizophrenic.

She wanted her mother to be rational enough to trust that she would never hurt her.

See me!

She wanted him to love her enough to stop being destructive.

She wanted him to be vulnerable and trust her to know that she would be worth it.

See me!

Mend. Mold. Alter. Change.

Everything felt better when it was earned.

She is evolving and shedding her skin, recreating herself.

Even now, in such a short time period, this disruption in her life has altered her and made her see things she needed to see.

She is starting to see herself from the inside out.

Decreasing the need, the blinding need, to control how everyone else sees her.

She is creating a new story, where her light is not diminished by her underground, by what she hides, but it is more brilliant because of it.

She is redirecting her intrigue, the beckoning mystery of uncertainty and gravitating it toward herself.

Where will she go?

What will she do?

With only herself to please?

But first, she wants to know peace in the beauty of now.

The mystery will unravel.

There will always be more to discover and more to repent.

Right now is full of acceptance and grace.

And she believes in it.

The Fog of Reality
Closes in.

The next day, she wakes up and stares absently at the quiet alarm clock; the grace of the weekend and her bed envelop her.

The fog closes in.

She remembers, and her heart drops, but artfully.

Something about this sadness is different.

It has a sweet taste to it that allures her.

She feels inspired and drawn to it and wants to keep it all to herself.

Love makes pain beautiful echoes.

She thought she loved him but now she doesn't know.

Maybe she loved the distraction, the effort.

She thought if she could conquer him, then surely she could conquer herself.

There it was, a secret agenda seeping its way into her life, undetected.

Misconceptions, nourished by fear, have led her to many dead ends and entanglements.

And yet, she still feels so much possibility, despite her efforts to self-destruct.

She lies there feeling different, as if she'd lost her virginity the night before.

Not sure how she should act and yet thankful for this disruption.

Change requires courage.

She has to get up, she has to keep moving, keep facing herself, opening up.

Drifting into the bathroom, she catches a glimpse of herself in the mirror, a glimpse that stops and holds her.

Does she look different?

Swollen with morning face and uneasiness, she searches her reflection for evidence of transformation. She wants to see what the rest of the world sees when they look at her.

He told me that he loved my face.

He could manipulate her so easily.

No matter what they were doing, she had always revealed herself to him, responded to him shamelessly.

She wanted him to see his effect, feel responsible for her feelings, so she could blame him when she wasn't happy.

Do you see what you've done?

She sees scary memories and sequences that illustrate her haunting thoughts.

His eyes, cold and dark. His energy, unaffected.

He was always nonchalant, inciting her more.

See me! Love me. Make me happy. Fill me. Lift me up.

He would run.

She would chase.

Embarrassment burns and she aches, never wanting this kind of exposure again.

But love makes pain beautiful and she can't help but see the beauty in her openness.

Despite her horror, there is a knowing.

She will always expose, she will always live for the thrill of raw emotion and she will always take the truth from it and leave the rest.

She has to feel it all, the expanse of her extremes so she can be a whole person.

She's learning to love this about herself and allow it.

Smile on it. Trust it.

Connect it to something bigger.

A swirling cocktail of emotions, a trust fall into greatness.

Personal and raw and experimental.

We're not supposed to be happy all the time and we are not meant to be perfect.

There will be upheaval.

There will be abuse and injustice.

But what looks bad today can turn around and bless tomorrow.

We can't avoid disappointment but we can reframe it.

Adversity pushes us to gain a firmer understanding of who we are.

The more you know about yourself, the less things bother you, the thicker your skin, and the more you understand the slant of others.

He was slanted toward survival and strategy.

She, toward spirit and feeling.

She suspects that he will always seek to minimize the risk of being split open, his secrets revealed.

He values his soul's privacy far more than he values the intimacy of sincere connection so he keeps his distance at any and all costs.

Intimacy would lead to his undoing—in his mind, an irrational and indulgent mistake.

There's always a deeper vibration than what seems apparent on the surface.

We choose our own misery, always, just as we choose our own happiness.

She's Ready to Hang Up.

Four rings. Five rings.

Relieved and disappointed, a dancing paradox in her belly.

Hello!

The voice is loud and shrill, devised to ward off persecutors.

Hi, Mommy—a timid greeting.

Gasp! *Is this my beautiful daughter?* Her pitch rises with each syllable, assaulting her daughter's ears, affecting her.

Yes, it's me. How are you?

Her tone and her words are calm, steady, practiced.

Her mother's state of mind is capricious.

It's a risk calling her unexpectedly, but she longs for her.

Even with the doom that will ultimately announce itself, she longs for the momentary happiness of her voice, her *my beautiful daughter*, her breathing, her sounds, her signs of contradiction and twists of mania.

This is her mother, her predicament, her matter of fact.

Her mother seems genuinely pleased to hear from her, and as if she was expecting her call, she immediately launches into a full-scale update on her life.

She has suspicious neighbors who watch her through the peephole and who do things to her at night with black magic.

She's making beautiful earrings in her jewelry class and she'll bring them the next time she visits.

She's shaved her hairline back several inches because she just couldn't seem to keep her hair out of her face.

The weather is beautiful.

She spoke to her father, he sounds well.

She keeps having allergic reactions, hives and rashes, some trouble breathing, but she has not seen a doctor.

As she talks, the words come faster, jumbling together, fighting to get out, squeezing and pushing past each other, a storm coming.

The daughter becomes exhausted, unable to ask her questions, listening for clues, trying to keep up, craving reciprocity and nurturing.

She can't find the words to comfort her mother or calm her.

She can picture her mother's face, her eyes darkening, her smile fading, distrust closing in.

> *Why are you calling? Did your father tell you to call? What do they want to know about me?*

> *No, no, nothing like that. I just wanted to hear your voice. I had a rough week. I caught my boyfriend cheating and I broke up with him and—*

She interrupts.

> *You've always been too trusting. These people out here will smile with their mouths and rape you with their eyes. I've always taught you that. Especially with me as your mother, you are a target. They might be listening to us right now. It's my fault. They bother you because of me. What have you told them?*

There's no stopping her now.

Her mother hears voices that no one else can hear and sees things that no one else can see.

Withdrawing, the daughter feels the familiar failure of trying to be mothered.

Reaching out, her hands blown off by friendly fire or mutilated by the sharp knives of accusation.

She tries, each effort less admirable than the last, until she can't anymore.

With every attempt to interject—to explain, justify, and pacify—her life force is depleted.

Self-preservation dictates and she retreats, anxious for the end of the phone call.

Every conversation, every visit, dies this way.

Resurrecting the fifteen-year-old girl, still trying to convince her mother that she didn't leave the oven on.

She never felt worthy, but if she could fix her mother, light up all of her hidden places, then that would prove to her that she was enough.

It always comes back to that.

Wide open, exposed to the severity of life and the complete surrender that it requires, she cries because she can't and she never could truly share her mother's reality.

Her smell, her voice, her softness.

Her arms, the safest place on earth.

Everything that made her tender.

Was it all just a dream to her?

The kind where you can remember sequences but not faces?

Fear but not love?

Life Keeps Requiring Things.

That she doesn't feel qualified to handle.

Every decision reveals another one yet to be made, and another and another.

Guilt clings to her peace.

She's fighting to feel free.

She's tired.

She does not like the person she becomes when her mother is in her life, yet her longing betrays her, compromises her.

Her childhood was shaped by chaos and love.

Her mother nurtured her and poured into her.

She taught her how to pray and be spiritual.

She showed her what happens when psychological disorders are mistaken for idiosyncrasies and are ignored.

Her mother and her mother's mother taught her what they knew, to enable her survival in the world.

She got lost looking for her mother, not recognizing herself as a being distinct from her.

When her mother went up, she went up.

When down, she went down.

Without her mother's distorted guidance and approval, she felt lost and always somewhat mistaken, so she wandered, seeking certainty.

Inside herself, in her intricacy, in her labyrinth, her mother is held, safe and untouchable.

Her softness, her sanity intact.

Everywhere else, she is danger and illness and emotional turmoil.

She gets lost in the dark places that exist between their two worlds.

Lost in the illusion that because of her mother, she can never be free.

Lost in the story she told herself for so long about the broken girl with the broken mother who would grow up to live a broken life.

She feels anxious after talking to her.

It's a chronic, sometimes dormant, but never-going-away anxiety.

It hinders her self-expression and casts a sinister shadow over any- and everything that is unknown.

Corrupts her imagination.

Steals the moments then the years.

When she was a child, her mother would be happy and playful one moment and inexplicably angry the next.

She heard voices.

She felt things her daughter didn't understand.

She lashed out.

Always alert to her episodes, she could sense when her mother's mood was changing, a storm coming.

She would resist and try to pull her back to a happy mother-daughter place.

But she couldn't keep here there, no matter how she tried.

She couldn't let go.

She blamed herself.

She suffered.

Attachment gave her anxiety.

It made her want to control things that she had no capacity to control, leaving her powerless and flailing bout.

Why would God create a world where you fall in love with people, places, and moments only to have them taken away?

A world where horrible things happen and you have to erase tragedy and loss from your mind and go about life as usual?

How is she to function when every moment, every happening is another and another good-bye?

Love makes pain beautiful.

To love life is to love freedom and be brave.

Love is not possession or blame.

She's getting into the habit of repeating affirmations to herself.

The landscape of the whole world is changing before her eyes.

This new, peculiar wisdom expands her sense of knowing, of regarding people.

Every day, every moment, people are shifting, pulled toward their own lessons.

They are not pulled toward or away from her, as a punishment, as if she is the great equilibrium.

Each of us is a whole universe, alive with our own realities, our worlds the reflections of our own minds.

If she is to love life and freedom and be brave, then she must learn to let go.

To see beauty without clinging to it, to feel pain without holding it hostage and to feel love without worry of losing it.

Her mind races with new thoughts and ways of being.

We Expect the World.

We paint our pictures and scenarios of how we want things to be, how we want people to behave and how we want to be perceived.

We worry and we stress over our expectations.

When they are not met, we feel unfavored.

We wish things were different.

We resist, draining our energy.

There is peace in accepting what is.

You wanted a sunny day but it is raining.

You wanted the job but you didn't get it.

You were generous and kind to those people and they repaid you with disregard.

You loved him and he didn't love you.

We want to see positive behavior rewarded and negative behavior punished.

When we don't, we become disillusioned and resentful.

Joy is repressed.

We can't find meaning.

What if we acted out of pure authenticity at all times, regardless of outcome?

What if we just loved for the sake of love itself?

What if we acted as if there is no other way to be, but to love and live and let go?

What if we adapted the ways of the constant witness inside of us, quietly observing everything, without judgment or expectation or resistance, simply noticing what *is*?

This is the world.

This is an angry person.

This is a happy person.

This is a rainy day.

This is a sick person.

This is a family.

This is humanity.

This is life.

This is death.

This is the world.

And this is where you stand in it.

You: with your ideas, your vibrations, and your intentions—the things you *can* control.

If we truly want freedom, we must let go of our expectations and embrace flow.

We will not always please and we will not always be pleased and we will still go on.

The more she accepts this reality without resistance, the more energy she can put toward appreciating what she has, without guilt.

Soul deep, she feels movement.

Her thoughts flow so naturally, as if she's always known.

Peace, her quiet muse, has been hiding in her labyrinth all along, just waiting to be discovered.

She Spots Her Friend.

Waiting for her on the park bench, transparent.

Uncertainty and angst visible through her smile.

As she walks toward her, she reminds herself of three things—love, truth, freedom.

She only needs those three intentions, and the right words will surely come out.

This is a defining moment.

Strained at best, their ten-year friendship has been off course for the last few months.

They hug and kiss, stand back and look each other up and down like women do.

Gushing over nails and outfits and smell goods.

A momentary high of feminine energy.

They sit down, both intent on finding their rhythm once again.

Their love is in the details.

The unspoken things.

The knowing acceptance.

The feeling of being witnessed and recognized and reflected effortlessly.

But lately, the details have been missing and the reflection has not been effortless.

Right away, as her friend begins to chatter away, the distance presents itself.

While once amused by her restlessness and her exploits, she now feels overwhelmed.

Her friend's stories are enactments, altered for the sake of the audience.

Truth and fiction commingled.

Image versus intimacy—their constant conflict.

She's bored by her friend's sameness.

The same stories of drama and confrontation.

The same victim mentalities.

The same obsession with status and money and sex.

Everything is a party.

Every whim—a pursuit.

Life is to be performed, not felt or authenticated.

She has always been drawn to this, the wounded exquisite.

Beauty, pain, signs of contradiction and twists of mania—a painful pattern.

She doesn't want the disapproval that she feels toward her, but it keeps bubbling up.

She wants the unconditional, the safe space they once created.

They made promises of friendship over marijuana highs and hangover lows, heartful agreements to never judge or criticize.

As her friend rambles on, she listens without caring.

She rejects her friend's hollow, meaningless anecdotes.

She keeps a steady, unsmiling gaze on her friend, revealing her speculation.

As soon as there is a pause, she fills the air with her own voice, leaning toward her, asking for something different.

Why do you act like you don't care about anything? You go from job to job, from man to man, and it's always someone else's fault.

She wants her friend's secret wishes, her underground, her labyrinth.

Beyond the shiny exterior, the labels and the show, she wants her feelings and her fears.

Do you ever take a moment to shake all that off and just feel what's really going on with yourself?

Maybe she used to talk the same talk, but over time and with her recent disruption fresh in her heart, she has become full of herself with knowing better and wanting more.

Is this what happens?

When you change your perspective of yourself, do you see your friends, relationships, career, *everything* differently?

She tries to explain.

I just don't care. Not about your plots for revenge or your silly arguments or how much money he makes. He treats you like shit and only sees you when he wants to have sex. You blame him in one breath, and in the next breath you brag about how much money he spends on you. Don't you want more for yourself?

Her idealism takes on its own presence, sitting between them on the bench, and neither of them can see around it.

She—caught up in its rapture.

Her friend—unnerved by its dismissal.

As the words come out of her mouth, her friend's eyes get bigger and bigger, and her mouth parts in disbelief.

There's a range of emotions, visible on her face, her inner witness revealed.

She watches her friend and waits, gives her space.

Talk to me. A silent plea, a last call to save them.

Sharp eyes, *I don't know what you're talking about. What do you mean you don't care? Since when do you think your life is so perfect and you can judge me?*

> *Ha! My life is not perfect! I know you must already know what's going on with me. He wasn't right, we weren't right, and I knew it and tried to force it anyway. I'm tired of pretending and forcing things. I'm ready to start being honest with myself. Aren't you? I can't sit here and have these same conversations with you. I want us to do better.*

Old ideas, limitations, sickness and loyalty.

Is she supposed to nod politely, giggle mischievously and pretend that her friend's façade is cute?

She can't.

> So you're judging me because your shit isn't working out? Everyone knew he was cheating; we tried to tell you, and you didn't want to listen. So now you want to bring me down with you? Make me feel bad about my choices? I don't need you to fix me.

Mend. Mold. Alter. Change.

She recalls their years of festivity.

Life was a party, and boys were the favors.

They got dressed up and got drunk.

They went on adventures and met boys and made them fall in love.

They got high and ran wild and they were free.

They rode fast and sung at the top of their lungs.

They were infinite and they crashed into each other.

They reveled in their reckless abandon.

There they were.

Clear in her mind, a vision of her former self, arm in arm with her partner in crime.

Now here sits her ex-partner, who she has made to feel unattractive and unwanted.

> *I'm sorry. I don't mean to be judgmental. But I was sinking. I was sinking fast. And the only thing that is saving me is being brutally honest with myself. I see you and I see us, how we used to be, and I don't know how to dismiss that life for me without dismissing it for you too. We raged, we did, and it was a time that needed to be had. But now I don't know how to want better for myself without wanting better for you too. I want to grow up and talk to you about growing up and reach new kinds of highs with you. Don't you want that?*

> *No, her friend says coldly. You're the stupid one, you're the bitter one, and you can keep all your 'wanting better' for yourself. You can't make me want what you want or be who you want me to be. You act like you are the first woman to be cheated on. It doesn't mean anything. Men cheat—that's what they do. If you want me to find some special meaning in it, I don't. If you think that you are a different person now and that you won't go back to letting people walk all over you, you're wrong. People are who they are, and there is no use trying to change. You've always been this way and now it's not good enough and you want to be different. As if being self-righteous will make you better off*

than me or help you escape life's bullshit. I can't even believe that you, of all people, are coming at me like this. Trust me: if he comes back to you and apologizes the right way, says the right things, you will take him back. That is what you do—it's what you always do, and I have never judged you for it.

She cringes. Is observing the same thing as judging?

I'm not judging. I just don't know how else to express what I'm going through right now without just saying it how I feel it. I'm not trying to attack you.

Sharp, hurt eyes. *Whatever. I didn't come here for this.*

They stared at each other for a moment, silently acknowledging the hole in the force field.

Whatever they had given each other, whatever they had been to each other feels inessential now.

Words unspoken, her friend gets up and walks away.

Her truth, raw and unsparing, is her only remaining companion.

The best company she's ever had.

And yet she feels messy and reckless, as if she just spilled a plate of food on herself to avoid crashing into a wall.

She looks around self-consciously.

She finds escape in watching people—jogging, walking, talking; children are playing, laughing, crying, jumping, and she is sitting on the bench with her clumsy honesty.

Her problems shrink when she considers the universe around her.

Perhaps she was judgmental.

Perhaps she was abrasive.

She couldn't be sure but she knows that she said how she felt.

She can't have it any other way anymore.

She considers her friend's prediction:

> *Trust me: if he comes back to you and apologizes the right way, says the right things, you will take him back. That is what you do—it's what you always do, and I have never judged you for it.*

She knows this time it is different and that she is on a new level.

No more starry-eyed enemy.

How could she ever take him back now that she knows better, now that she's learning to love and accept herself?

She could never go back to that.

She sits on the bench, afternoon into evening, thinking about it, convincing herself.

She could never go back to that.

She could never go back to that.

She Fears She Will Have to Lose Everyone.

In order to save herself.

She has turned all her conversations inward.

In such a short amount of time, she has come to enjoy her solitude, her reflective space—so much that she has distanced herself from everyone.

Monopolized by transformation, she has created her own cocoon.

And she wonders if she will be hard to love, because she is so consumed with and comforted by her own little world.

Perhaps she was too harsh with her friend.

She feels small for making assumptions and big for taking a stand.

She thought she would be fulfilled with every declared truth and loved and understood by everyone who mattered.

This was the heavenly destination she sought.

The promised land.

She felt so good in the moment, changing the conversation and participating in her own truth for a change.

But now she knows there is an art to it.

This won't be the last time she has to disappoint someone to avoid betraying herself.

She so dutifully diminished herself all her life.

Wanting everyone to feel comfortable all the time, even at her own expense.

Being passive and undecided, going with the flow in order to be less of a burden.

Not wanting to disagree or cause conflict, she let whatever was happening—happen.

Now here, after making herself visible, she feels strengthened.

Her promised land won't be perfect, everyone won't get it, and some will reject her, think she's weird.

But things are not always what they seem.

She'd been reliant on the wrong kind of tension, the kind that comes from inner conflict and self-denial.

Intrigued by uncertainty, trying to control the uncontrollable through accommodation, trial and error. Her mother, her lover, her friends.

Here, in her cocoon, somehow she knows she is not really alone despite how isolated she feels.

She is releasing an old way of thinking, moving forward with an open heart and mind.

It Hurts to Become.

So much so that we avoid it altogether.

We avoid the journey within because it might hurt.

It might leave a mark.

It might change us.

We might fail.

We might succeed.

They might not like it.

We will have to let some things go.

People may misunderstand our intentions.

Our first efforts might be clumsy.

But we must first accept our own realities in order for others to accept them.

If the goal is to do everything with love and sincerity, then we must clearly articulate our true feelings.

We are always concerned about what *they* will say.

They say we can't do it.

They say how we've messed up in the past.

They say that this is right and this is wrong.

They say all kinds of things, don't they?

They know what's best.

They know what we should be afraid of, what we should look like and how we should feel.

God forbid they see us fall or they don't like us or they see our humanity.

Heaven help us.

What would we do then?

Would the earth open up and consume us?

Would the sky open up and pour down its wrath?

Or would we learn to thrive in it?

To be inspired by rejection.

To find strength in vulnerability.

She needs this tension, this creative space to realize her potential and grow.

To stop proving and start being.

This disruption is vivid.

Nothing will stay hidden now that she is here.

There is more to discover and share.

Going deeper, touching everything and allowing everything to touch her.

Leaning in to See the Computer Screen.

She can smell the salesman's breath and see the swollen, ingrown hairs on his cheek.

Is he self-conscious about these things?

He thanks her for being patient, tells her that she is his second customer ever; his eyebrows and upper lip are sweaty.

She wants him to feel comfortable.

Everyone won't be patient with him, but I will be, she decides.

She thinks about her breath, her blemishes, her insecurities.

She wonders why these things distract her so much from living.

She doesn't want anyone to see her flaws, so she finds herself curious about those who have theirs out in the open, unashamed, for all to see.

She sees the beauty in it, the freedom.

How many times has she been self-conscious, uncertain of her appearance or her knowledge, choosing to stay silent or run away when she could have contributed something meaningful?

Always thinking that her existence would be a burden to someone.

Her appearance, off-putting. Her input, irrelevant.

She has been here before, in this store, holding hands with her love.

Feeling slightly uncomfortable, never certain of where she stood with him.

She had seen the signs of his indifference countless times and she had ignored all the warnings.

Self-conscious, blaming herself, she thought she could do something, change in some way, to make him love her more.

Too sensitive.

No conviction.

Self-disgust.

When she felt too much, she would stutter, showing her discomfort and insecurity; she didn't feel safe.

He grew weary of her delicacy.

That's how she makes sense of it.

He wanted her to require more of him and when she did not, he looked for intrigue elsewhere.

She wanted to be different, someone other than herself.

More vocal, more demanding, more assertive.

Whatever it was he needed, that was what she wanted to be.

And here now, even with her resolve and her new ways of thinking and being, she still wishes she were different.

She wonders, what if?

Her mind never stops.

She's growing, she's awakening, then she's regressing.

She hates that she's still thinking about what she could have done to keep him.

Ma'am? Is this the one? The salesman interrupts her thoughts.

She likes him.

He is informative and thorough.

His nervousness, endearing.

He knows most things, admits what he doesn't—eager to serve and figure out.

The encounter reminded her that she doesn't have to look or smell or be perfect in order to be worthy.

She finds herself looking for inspiration in everyday people, everyday things, all day.

Just like she made up her mind to be patient and kind to the salesman, there will be people in her life who will make up their minds to mistreat her.

But she can walk away.

She can teach others how to treat her and she can decide what she welcomes into her space.

Love and self-preservation.

She's not a victim, apologizing and begging for mercy; she has choices and she can't lose anything that is meant for her.

All day she wanders, a face among many, her thoughts giving her companionship and insight.

The world seems to be conspiring to teach her.

At the supermarket, she smiles at the cashier.

The cashier's face lights up in response.

I've been working for hours and you are the first person to smile at me. Thank you.

A gentle reminder.

Kindness is not a weakness.

At the post office, a woman walking toward the entrance carrying too many packages drops everything on the ground.

Cursing and flustered, the contents of her purse spill out as she leans over to pick up the packages.

She goes over to help her.

The woman allows her to help but doesn't thank her, walks away still cursing under her breath.

She smiles to herself.

An unexpected reward.

She doesn't need acknowledgment to feel good about her actions.

She runs into a friend at the gym.

She hasn't been returning this friend's calls or text messages.

There are questions in her eyes.

She explains that she's going through some things and needs some time to herself.

Ahhhh. She gets it.

The questions are answered without words.

Unspoken acceptance.

The familiar feeling of being witnessed and recognized and reflected effortlessly.

A loving affirmation.

Love doesn't cling or try to control.

Love doesn't try to satisfy itself.

Love lets you breathe.

She's sitting in traffic, she's negotiating with her landlord, she's eating lunch, she's observing, she's interacting and she's learning.

She's watching herself, noticing herself.

She's seeing the world through new eyes.

She's deciding.

She doesn't want to be anyone else.

She wants to be exactly herself—sensitive, open, real—and comfortable in her own skin.

She gives thanks that day, in her mind, in her heart, with her whole being, for discovering an enduring passion for peace of mind, resolved that she will eliminate anything that threatens it.

It may hurt to be rejected.

But it hurts so much more to reject yourself.

We aspire to greatness to achieve our goals.

It's pushed in our faces every day: *Live Your Best Life! Get Organized! Find the Love of Your Life in Thirty Days!*

But in the pursuit of our best, we often reject who we are today.

We compare ourselves.

We can't stop.

We make unreasonable assumptions, trying to measure up.

We are obsessed with how people see us and where we fit in.

Now she is eliminating the ideas of who she ought to be.

And she's falling in love with who she *is*.

Her labyrinth, her underground—a place of wholeness, not shame.

Triggers.

The next day, without warning, she finds herself undone.

Feeling sorry for herself and alone.

Last night was the hardest.

Her fear was the loudest.

She's tired.

She's weak, crazy in her blood.

It always comes back to that.

She doesn't tell her story; her story tells her, and she plays the role.

Autopilot—destiny and composition.

It started with a phone call from her mother.

She ignored the call and welcomed the guilt.

She couldn't give her access.

The doom would ultimately announce itself.

Removing herself from her mother hurts her.

It's not what she's supposed to do.

But it's what she has to do.

She feels the weight of her sacrifice.

She wants revenge.

She tries to gather herself into one feeling that will simplify everything.

All she can come up with is vengeance.

She asks herself bottomless questions, her thoughts stormy, her mind a fair-weather friend.

Is this how it's going to be?

One day, inspired and aglow with enlightenment; the next day, angry and resentful.

Today everything has a black cloud over it.

Her thoughts turn to his lies, her allowances.

At church, the minister preaches about revenge.

How appropriate.

She predicts the message.

Forgive and forget, turn the other cheek.

The person who forgives is stronger than the person who retaliates.

Spiritually, this feels right.

But in this moment, something has shifted.

She can't see the brighter side, the lessons and the growth and the becoming.

It feels wrong that he's allowed to think that he's right, that he won.

How can she allow that? Where is his punishment?

This is not the inspiring, sweet-tasting sadness that allured her; this is the bitter sadness that feels slippery and dangerous and unsustainable.

She's back in flux.

Everything she knows about herself—her journey, her intricacy, her becoming—is swallowed up by his betrayal.

Her feelings are a virtual mind map in her head, triggering thoughts and assumptions that she can't control.

His sin is her burden.

Everyone pities her and knows her weaknesses.

She made herself vulnerable for him and now she sees judgment everywhere.

Her embarrassment leads her to anger.

He gets to look like the winner.

He lied.

He cheated.

He took advantage of her.

Now he is free and she is trapped in a bitter cage.

Her anger leads to fear.

No protection.

She aches, never wanting this kind of exposure again, fearing that her heart will break over and over and over, a slow leak with no chance to heal.

Her body and spirit exposed to deception.

Intimacy contaminated.

Her fear leads to suffering.

She can't accept his betrayal and disregard.

Not today.

She can't find the strength.

Today, she wants revenge.

She wants to dig a deep hole and get dirty and ugly and be the winner.

She pictures herself screaming and crying, throwing love in his face.

Images float and agony squeezes and won't let go.

Her suffering leads to sadness.

Finally, the tears come.

Discreetly She Weeps.

Eyes full, throat swollen, face hot.

The minister says the best way to get revenge is to open your heart, choose love and forgive.

Bitterness is toxic and will eat you up.

Underneath her rage, the knowing is quiet.

Her constant witness—patient and understanding.

Abiding through her extremes.

Paying attention but not possessing.

She doesn't have to be happy all the time or judge her feelings as good or bad.

She knows that people who are hurting will hurt other people.

He doesn't know how to share anything but his pain.

Removing herself from him is revenge enough.

Creating love and light from a sudden disruption, an awakening slap.

Her revenge is choosing to be free.

His face pops into her mind, aloof and full of disdain.

She wants to get up and leave.

She feels exposed here in church with her conflicts.

She was raised to care about right and wrong, good and bad, heaven and hell.

But her heart has always drawn her toward a broader reverence, forcing her to find out for herself.

Can she see her darkness, dive into it headfirst, swim to the bottom of it and still rise back to the top?

An abiding sense of hope, betraying her misery and self-punishments, underlies her current fury.

She looks from side to side, fearing that her inner battle is obvious.

But she is contained, as always.

Her passion burns inside.

She is uncomfortable, bloated, with all that she holds.

She feels peculiar and vulnerable and she wonders what everyone else is going through.

Breathe. Steady. Release.

Everything but love is temporary.

She bends but she doesn't break.

Her Matter of Fact.

Doubt has come calling.

Perhaps it never left.

She hears voices.

They tell her that she's aware, she is resourceful, and she has the ability to choose.

There is also a dark voice, a critic, intent on downplaying her enthusiasm.

Questioning her at every turn.

She has fallen a step behind, and now she wanders, intrigued by shadows.

What she fears most is that despite her empowering guidance, she will choose badly—revenge and bitterness—a victim of destiny and composition.

She just doesn't trust herself yet.

But she knows how she wants to feel.

Free.

Free to create her own story, instead of her story telling her who to be, what to feel, how to act.

To be a girl, content with her thoughts and her choices.

Mistakes with no regrets.

To know that life is rich and complicated and her emotions are relevant.

To stand with outward composure and inner acceptance— magnetic, surrounded by love.

She reflects upon her life, then the last few days and the product of that time, which is her present, her matter of fact.

The story she told herself about the broken girl with the broken mother who would grow up to live a broken life.

The disruption—his betrayal and his indifference.

Her determination, her knowing, her journey calling.

The painful memories, her underground, full of wrinkles and treasures.

The yearning and resentment—a paradox dancing in her belly.

The quiet acknowledgment, the affirmation, the pot of devotion.

Clumsy actualizations, realized and spoken.

Her truth, raw and unsparing, her only companion.

Her, waiting and expecting in vain for her mother's mania to magically cease.

Her, waiting and expecting in vain for a man to fill her up, to validate her.

She sighs, feeling heavy.

Tomorrow will be a new day.

A way of being, specifically designed for that day, will present itself.

She wonders who she will be.

She Doesn't Know Exactly Why.

But today is different.

She feels unstoppable.

She wakes up that morning with the fog, the knowing, the empty bed and the silence, but she welcomes it.

She's been staying home from work.

Mending her heart and soul.

After a few difficult days, she feels once again certain that the disruption was a good thing, not just trying-to-convince-herself good, but heartfelt good, a calmness settled in her core.

She is out of the house by sunrise, convinced the world is waiting for her.

All day, she feels it.

She practically dances through her day and everyone she encounters feels her rapture.

Nothing can go wrong.

Everything is new and she is aglow.

She savors her morning walk as if it were her first or her last.

She commits to her work lovingly.

She eats her lunch with reverence, picturing the food nourishing her body, and she feels gratitude.

Her five senses are renewed and expanded, awake to any and all inspiration and happy feelings.

This clarity, strange but familiar, has been there all along, buried and overlooked.

Her life is full of miracles and spectacles that she has been afraid to rely on.

For so long she didn't know how to enjoy, how to be thankful, without guilt.

But now, clarity feels clean and effortless.

Why resist peace? Why deny herself?

Waiting for something to be given that she can give to herself.

She's weary of the alarm system in her head, the dread that was always with her, alert to her next disaster.

She has decided to appreciate everything.

She knows she cannot control every thought, every feeling but she can decide which ones to feed.

And with that knowledge comes all kinds of confidence, and yes, clarity.

Peace will be her life's work.

Mistakes. Success. Excitement. Boredom. Pleasure. Pain.

All necessary.

Peace of mind is a choice.

The alternative is chronic dissatisfaction, a stain that can be covered up but not removed.

The unappreciative eye can only see the distance between what it has and what it wants.

Restricted by tunnel vision.

The beauty is missed.

Looking at the same closed door.

The same man.

The same past.

The same patterns.

As we fight and kick and scream.

No matter what yesterday was like, this moment is hers.

Her now wants her, it craves her attention, ready to go deeper and connect with her.

She's into it.

She's into this new now that has descended upon her.

She knows something about herself and the sparkle in her eye declares her.

There is a wonderful release that comes from making peace with a nightmare.

The fog clears.

She sees the smoke and mirrors for what they are.

Clarity came when she realized that she could decide—how she wants to feel, how she wants to think, and how she wants to live her life.

This is the best day ever.

The kind that you don't share with anyone.

She's in her zone, where no one can touch her or understand her quiet significance.

It's only for her, as some things should be.

Just a few days ago, she was shattered, swallowed up by rejection and loss.

Life interrupted.

A beautiful disruption.

Her now is offering her a beautiful day and she feels like she deserves it.

She considers where she is and where she wants to go.

She is moving away from regret and self-doubt.

She is moving against pretenses and expectations.

She is moving with free will, grace and humility.

She's finding the joy in the ride.

She pulls into her parking lot after a day of peaceful travels and meaningful moments.

She sees a familiar SUV in the spot next to hers.

Her heart stops.

Why is He Here?

Helplessly, she pulls into her spot, hands trembling, heart pounding in her ears.

Everything.

Gone.

Out the window.

Just like that.

Wait.

What is he doing here?

Just when she'd stopped rehearsing what she would say to him.

Just when she'd started to feel free, at least the beginnings of it, he shows up, as if he has some kind of radar.

She wants to appear cold and unaffected, the only way to be in this situation.

She parks and gets out of the car and boldly walks around his car and approaches his window.

A deliberate look—*what do you want?*—on her face.

He gets out of the car and stands in front of her, chin down, head tilted to the side, eyes peering out under long lashes, beckoning—his usual stance when he's enticing her.

> *Hi. I'm sorry for not calling, but I knew you would tell me not to come.*

Did you leave something in the house? She's looking at his beard and the way it frames his lips.

Why is this happening?

Slipping dreadfully into autopilot, she struggles to appear still and calm.

His height and the tilt of his head and how her eyes are level with his lips framed by that beard.

This is impossible.

> *Can we just talk?*

> *No, there's nothing to talk about.*

I'm really ready to talk now. I will answer your questions. I'm sorry.

Sorry? For what? Why are you sorry now? I don't want to talk.

His unexpected appearance tempts her with power.

She's always wanted the upper hand, and now she has it.

The look in his eyes, the remorse, the helplessness—this is the face and the feeling she craved when he dismissed her and laughed at her so recklessly.

Time seems to have stopped as they stand there silently interacting, something familiar happening.

It's a standoff.

He has this way of washing over her, making her lose her balance.

She stands there daring him to convince her, to make her feel him, knowing that his entire attention will dissolve her.

She does not like the person she becomes when he is in her life, yet her longing to prove herself betrays her, compromises her resolve.

He is a threat to her peace, a sweet taboo that distorts her *now*—her beautiful, promising *now*.

The now that wants her and craves her attention, ready to go deeper.

He is and always will be a flight risk.

It should be an easy choice.

But really, must she choose?

Can't she keep her peace *along* with his delicious turmoil?

Can't she go her own way without leaving him behind?

> *I know. I'm sorry. Okay, you don't have to talk. Can you just hear what I have to say?*

It's happening again.

Autopilot.

This feels out of style.

She says no, he says yes; he humbles, she softens.

They don't do *her* way, they do *his* way.

She's watching herself walk him toward the door, fumbling around in her purse, trying to locate her resolve.

Then she's opening the door.

She's going back to that place, the habit, the perpetual loop.

Where did her power go?

She watches herself let him in the house.

Telling him she'll be right in.

She sits down on the step, of the porch, of the house, where they'd loved, kissed, laughed and fought.

She feels like her own starry-eyed enemy.

A victim of destiny and composition.

Tempted to delight in escape, knowing that she will suffer when she returns to herself and finds chaos.

Wait.

Soul deep, she feels movement.

She woke up feeling unstoppable.

And something else.

Gloriously human.

Illuminated.

Unpredictable.

Now, he's here.

And she can't help but wonder what he has to say.

How hard she falls for a beautiful moment, a tender distraction.

An apology, a revealing of souls, no illusions, their wild hearts revealed.

She's preoccupied with sensation as the sky falls down around her.

She has to feel it all, the expanse of her extremes, so she can be whole.

She takes chances, chases chaos, all efforts to avoid a default life.

But this is a new story.

She has explored the longing and the fear in the core of her being.

She has confronted herself without flinching or hiding or covering up.

Setting her judgments aside.

Evoking all-encompassing love, unleashed and spilling over.

Her impulses don't surprise her anymore, blowing her this and that way.

She recognizes the swing, the familiar back and forth.

Right. Wrong. Good. Bad.

What she should do and what she shouldn't do.

Suddenly, she laughs out loud to herself.

It doesn't matter what he says or what she says or if she gives him another chance or not.

What matters is that she doesn't make decisions out of fear anymore, out of limitation and defeat.

She will face her choices with self-awareness and ownership.

Ready to accept the possibilities that result.

What matters is that she is not afraid to show up and show herself, to participate in her own truth.

Life, her soulful adventure, calls her to enjoy the ride.

This is how she will live out her questions now.

Consciously.

Courageously.

Clumsily, if necessary.

She hears voices like her mother did but they tell her that she is whole and she can trust herself.

She is her own witness and her own defiance.

Love makes pain beautiful, when a broken heart serves as the ultimate path to freedom.

Epilogue: From A Whisper to A Roar.

You can suppress and deny all you want.

The lessons you need to learn will still find you.

You can pretend you don't care.

Tell yourself that you're a realist and that having a dream is a waste of time.

Acquire things that don't fulfill you and wonder why you feel empty.

Believe that life's a bitch and then you die.

Numb your way through life.

You can see your life as a to-do list instead of an adventure.

Busy yourself with busyness.

Be predictable, afraid of change.

Stubborn, afraid of growth.

Resist the urge to explore.

Never turn left instead of right, just to try something different.

Never get up on the bar and dance.

Take your life for granted.

Focus all your attention on lack.

Overlook your blessings and cry about what's missing.

Obsess over closed doors.

Don't value what you are, only value what you are not.

Tell yourself you'll be happy after you get what you want.

Don't celebrate now.

Wait for everything to be perfect.

Save your good panties for a special occasion.

Buy your favorite perfume and never wear it.

Deny yourself simple pleasures.

Live in a dollhouse with pretty things, fake smiles and no emotion.

You can cling to the past.

Its relationships, its pain, its pleasure, its illusions.

Don't appreciate the here and now.

You can spend time with toxic people.

Let them fill your mind with their fears and limitations.

Get sucked in.

Drink their poison.

Feel sick.

Put out your flame so as not to shine in their darkness.

Don't say what you need to say.

Hold in your true feelings.

Say you're okay when you're not.

Hide it all away.

Bury it.

Die with it.

You can be judgmental.

Make assumptions and be defensive.

Criticize others the way you criticize yourself all day, every day.

If you can't escape it, then why should they?

Beat yourself up daily.

Don't forgive yourself.

Live in fear of making a mistake.

Attack from all angles—call yourself names, eat your feelings, let people mistreat you, abuse money.

Kill, kill, kill.

Spend your life looking for someone to complete you, someone to fix.

Believe you aren't whole by yourself and that you can't be in love with yourself.

Settle for whoever will take you because it's better than being alone.

Envy your neighbor.

Compare yourself and count everyone's blessings before your own.

Tell yourself that you have bad luck and are worse off than everyone else.

Believe that your life would be better if you were someone else.

Hold grudges.

Don't let anything go.

Don't let anyone get anything over on you ever.

Always have the last word.

Punish and destroy.

Wear a mask.

Change yourself to receive approval.

Be overly responsible, be everything to everyone, until you self-destruct.

Don't discover yourself.

Avoid the journey within.

Believe that your flesh and bones are all that you are.

This world—all that there is.

About the Author

GG Renee Hill is a writer and blogger under the influence of three children and a passion for soulful living. She writes about all the many layers that make women the beautiful contradictions that they are. Her blog, *All the Many Layers*, is a resource for women who yearn to create more meaningful experiences in their everyday lives.

She has learned from experience that growth comes from making mistakes and taking imperfect action. There will be times when the past comes back to haunt, self-doubt distracts and we can't seem to get out of our own way. Through her blog and her books, GG's mission is to explore these nuances and encourage women to connect with each other through storytelling and creative expression.

She believes that the way you live your life is your art and your message to the world. You can stay abreast of her future projects through her blog and social media platforms.

Blog: www.allthemanylayers.com

Twitter and Instagram: @ggreneewrites

Facebook: www.facebook.com/ggreneewrites

Special thanks to Jennifer Arnise (www.mysoulfly.com) for the cover art and to Carl Chester (C Dot Chester Photography) for the author photo.

Made in the USA
Lexington, KY
17 October 2016